TERRIBLE, TERRIBLE!

A FOLKTALE RETOLD

by ROBIN BERNSTEIN

Pictures by
SHAUNA MOONEY KAWASAKI

KAR-BEN
PUBLISHING
www.karben.com
800-4KARBEN

The author thanks Judye Groner, Lesléa Newman, Rabbi Bob Saks, and Madeline Wikler for their generous help in bringing this book to fruition.

For Heidi Creamer
who creates art, laughter, and joy in her very little house.
–R.B.
To Bonnie R. W., and all who belong to her.
–S.M.K.

Kar-Ben Publishing
A division of Lerner Publishing Group, Inc.
241 First Avenue North
Minneapolis, MN 55401 U.S.A.
1-800-4KARBEN

www.karben.com

Library of Congress Cataloging-in-Publication Data

Bernstein, Robin
   Terrible, terrible! : (a retold folktale) / Robin Bernstein : Illustrated by
Shauna Mooney Kawasaki
      p.   cm
   Summary: In this contemporary retelling of the classic Jewish folktale,
a rabbi advises a blended family how to deal with their overcrowded house.
   ISBN 1-58013-016-X (hardcover) . — ISBN 1-58013-017-8 (pbk.)
   1. Jews—Folklore. 2. Folklore.) I. Kawasaki, Shauna Mooney, ill.
II Title.
PZ8.1.B4177Tg 1998
398.2'084'924—dc21 (E)   98-11484

Manufactured in the United States of America
1 – VI – 11/1/09

"I'll love you forever," Abigail's mother said. But she wasn't talking to Abigail.

"I'll always love you, too," said Abigail's new stepfather, and they slid rings on each other's fingers. Together they stamped on a glass wrapped in a dishtowel, and everyone shouted, "MAZEL TOV!"

But Abigail didn't shout. She bit her lip, as she always did when she was worried. Right after the wedding, she and her mom would move in with her new stepfather and four new stepsisters and brothers. Seven people in all. Abigail was the youngest.

Living with so many people wasn't easy. Every time Abigail wanted to use the bathroom, someone was already in it. If she wanted to watch TV, someone had already tuned it to a different channel. If she had her heart set on an apple, someone had already eaten the last one. And worst of all, there was no place for Abigail to be alone.

"This house is too small!" she complained to her mother. "Every corner is stuffed with people and junk!"

"We can't afford a bigger home," said Abigail's mom.

"We can't get rid of the people," said her stepfather, "and I like the junk."

"If I come up with some ideas, will you try them?" Abigail asked.

"I promise we will," her mom said.

"Yes," her stepdad agreed. "This house is a little cramped for my taste, too."

The wisest person Abigail knew was the rabbi. The rabbi could solve any problem, big or small. She could bless a baby, console the bereaved, and sing a tune so beautiful that all who heard it would rise to their feet and dance. Abigail was sure the rabbi could help her.

"Rabbi," Abigail said, "I have a problem. My mother and stepfather and my four new brothers and sisters and I live in a tiny house. Everyone's crammed in so tight, I can't walk across the room without tripping over my brother's feet or my sister's knees. But there's no money for a bigger home. Rabbi, what should I do?"

The rabbi thought deeply. Then she spoke.

"Do you and your siblings have any bicycles?" she asked.

"Sure," said Abigail. "And so do my parents. We keep them in the garage."

"Bring them into the house," said the rabbi.

"But there's no room!" Abigail cried. "The house will burst at the seams and fall in a pile of match sticks!"

"Trust me," said the rabbi. "Bring the bicycles into the house."

So Abigail dragged all seven bicycles into the tiny house. She placed two in the kitchen, one against the refrigerator, the other against the stove. She found room for two more in the living room stacked on top of the couch. She balanced one in the hall and hung one from the ceiling. The last, she parked in the bathtub.

"This is what the rabbi advised?" Abigail's mother asked. "Maybe she was joking."

"The rabbi does like jokes," Abigail answered. "But I think she was serious this time. Remember, you promised to try my ideas."

"We did promise," her stepfather said grimly, and they let the bicycles stay.

By the next day, everything was worse. There was no place to cook or read or bathe or have a civilized conversation.

"Rabbi," said Abigail, "I know I only saw you yesterday, but today I'm thinking maybe I misunderstood you. I brought the bicycles into the house, but it's terrible, terrible, worse than before! Rabbi, what should I do?"

The rabbi thought for a long moment, then asked, "Do you have any pets?"

"Yes," said Abigail. "We have three cats and two dogs, a rabbit and a guinea pig. We keep them in the backyard."

"Bring them into the house."

"Rabbi!" Abigail gasped. "There's no room! The house will splinter into sawdust and pipes!"

But the rabbi would not budge.

When Abigail's mother came home and found her letting the guinea pig loose in the kitchen, her mother shouted, "If the rabbi isn't joking, then she's playing a cruel trick!"

"The rabbi is fond of tricks," Abigail answered. "But she said this will help us."

"Our home will be ruined!" yelled her mother. And she appeared to be right. The dogs raced all over the house, whisking toys off the shelves with their wagging tails. The cats clawed the furniture. The bunny and guinea pig were nowhere to be found, but signs of them were everywhere.

"Rabbi," said Abigail, "yesterday I did as you advised. But terrible, terrible, worse than before! The dogs bark, the cats meow, and the rabbit and guinea pig are suspiciously quiet. We're smooshed together like pickles in a jar. Rabbi, what should I do?"

The rabbi thought hard and asked. "Do you have any cousins?"

"Yes," said Abigail. "Dozens of cousins."

"Invite them to visit," said the wise rabbi.

"You can't be serious," said Abigail. But the rabbi was.

When Abigail confessed that she had invited all the cousins to stay, her mother bellowed, "I changed my mind! This rabbi isn't joking, and she isn't playing a trick! She's crazy, pure and simple!"

"Sometimes the wisest people seem crazy," Abigail answered, but even she was beginning to have her doubts.

"I know we promised to try your ideas," her mother said, "but…" a rumble drowned out the sound of her mother's voice. It was the sound of a thousand stomping feet.

"HELLO!" shouted the cousins as they poured into the house.

"Oof," said Abigail, as a cousin stepped on her toe.

"Ack," said her stepfather, as another cousin elbowed him in the stomach. The cousins were marching in, unstoppable as a spring flood. Twenty cousins crammed into the living room, fifteen more stuffed into the kitchen, and eight jammed in the bathroom. They ate every bit of food, played loud music, and danced until dawn.

The next day, Abigail's mother called out weakly.

"Please Abigail," she begged, "please send the cousins away."

"I'm going back to the rabbi." Abigail said, although it was difficult to inflate her lungs enough to speak. Abigail climbed over the dozens of cousins and escaped through the bathroom window.

"Rabbi," Abigail wheezed, flexing her numb arms and legs. "Rabbi, I took your advice, but it's terrible, terrible, worse than before! The house is so crowded, I can't lift my hand to wipe away my tears. I hear the cats and dogs crying, but I can't look for them because I can't move a single step. My family has disappeared under piles of bicycles, pets, and cousins. The walls moan, the floors groan, and I'm scared the beams will split. Rabbi, please help us before we lose everything. And don't ask me to add something new, because there's not room for a toothpick more."

The wise rabbi smiled. "Tell your cousins to go home," she said. "Take your three cats and your two dogs, your rabbit and your guinea pig, and return them to the backyard. Walk your seven bicycles to the garage. Find your family and cook a meal together. Eat it, then clean up together."

"Oh, Rabbi," said Abigail, "that's just what I hoped you would say."

So Abigail returned to her house, which was growing round like a balloon about to burst. She opened the front door, and eighteen cousins spilled out.

"Excuse me! Pardon me!" Abigail shouted as she elbowed her way into the living room, where the cousins were still dancing. Abigail picked up the radio and started a conga line. The cousins joined hands and followed her as she danced them through the living room, down the hall, and finally out the front door. Then Abigail handed the radio to a tall cousin and she watched as the crowd danced joyously down the street and into the twilight.

Abigail found her mother and her stepfather and her four brothers and sisters. They were slightly dented, but unharmed. The three cats and two dogs, the rabbit and the guinea pig crept out cautiously. Everyone walked a bicycle back to the garage. Then they went to the market and each chose one thing to eat: a loaf of bread, carrots, peanut butter, pickles, apples, and grape juice. Abigail chose graham crackers.

When they got back to the house, the door swung open easily. "Nothing's blocking it," Abigail marveled.

They brought the food into the kitchen and laid it out. "Look how much space there is," Abigail's mother said. "Our food fits on the table. And we have enough chairs for all of us."

After dinner, everyone cleaned up. Abigail mopped the kitchen and said, "I never realized how big this floor was." Her stepfather swept the hall, which now seemed cavernous. Her siblings picked up the fallen toys and books, and her mother scrubbed the bicycle grease out of the bathtub.

"Maybe we should let the pets back in," Abigail suggested, and everyone thought that was a marvelous idea. They brought back the three cats and the two dogs, the rabbit and the guinea pig, and everyone agreed that their lives were wonderful, wonderful, better than ever.